Playing

Pretend

I0562128

Alyse Zaftig

Out

Jude

"You're done."

"What?" I couldn't believe my ears. "What did you say?"

"You heard me. You are off the team."

"I can't be off the team. My scholarship depends on being on the football team. Come on. Can't you just bench me?"

"No. You got caught drinking, and you're only 20. There's no way that I could keep you on the team, even if I wanted to. The Indianapolis Star has picked up the story of you and the other boys who got caught. What on earth possessed you to spray paint graffiti on one of the university buildings?"

"Hey, I spent the last weekend

cleaning all that off. Come on, I paid my dues. I'm sorry! I was drunk."

"Our football team can't afford players who drag us down. There's no room for you on this team."

"What am I going to do? I love football. How am I going to stay in school if I don't have my scholarship?"

"You should've thought of that before you drank and vandalized university property. This is part of being an adult; you have to own your mistakes and deal with the consequences. Now get out of my office. I don't have any more time for you."

My shoulders slumped as I walked slowly out of my coach's office. The only reason why I could even afford to go to college was my football scholarship. Neither of my parents had graduated from college, and my athletic ability was my only ticket out of Jasper,

Indiana. If I didn't have my scholarship, I needed to come up with enough money to stay here. What was I going to do? Finals were coming up soon, and I needed to pay my tuition by two weeks afterwards. Even if I could find a job right now, I wouldn't be able to make enough money. Additionally, there was no chance that I would pass my finals if I was working a full-time job trying to make enough money to pay for my tuition.

Men didn't cry. I told myself that as I walked home. I would lose my apartment. All of the athletes lived near the training facilities, but now that I was off the team, I'd have to move out. I hoped that they would let me stay there until the end of the semester, but where was I going to live? All of the apartments in Bloomington were rented for a year beginning in August. I had no idea how I was going to afford an apartment, let alone find one.

I went home to my apartment, and then I jumped into the shower after turning on the fan. The warm water calmed me down. It washed away all of my stress. Inside of the shower, I could think more clearly.

All I needed to do was find a job that would be flexible enough for me to stay in school. It needed to pay enough money for me to afford tuition, as well as my living expenses.

As I got out of the shower, I caught sight of myself in the mirror. It was a little foggy, but I wiped the condensation off with my towel.

I wasn't male model material, but I wasn't ugly, either. I had certainly been successful enough with women in high school and college, although I didn't know how much of that was being a football player.

I flexed. After spending most of

my life playing sports, my body surely was worth something.

I thought about stripping, but I discarded the idea. There was only one strip club in Bloomington, and it only had female strippers. No, if I wanted to make money, I would need to find something else.

I wrapped my towel around my waist and got out my laptop. I had gotten it as part of my scholarship, and I was glad that they wouldn't take it away, at least. The university wi-fi was hit or miss, despite the university being featured as one of the most wired campuses in the United States by *Wired*. This time, it worked.

I scrolled through Craigslist. Sure, it was full of crazy people, but this was the way that I found all of my jobs in college. In a small town, everybody knew each other. Bloomington might be a little bit bigger, but I was sure that I would find something that wasn't too sketchy.

The first job post that I saw said that I could get paid to go to church. I clicked on it to read through the description. They had a company that paid for evaluations of experiencing the inside of a church for the first time. I shook my head. That wouldn't fit for me. I had not been inside of one since I was confirmed.

I saw another one that had

part-time, seasonal positions at Indiana University. They only made about $10 an hour. That would never be enough for me to pay for my tuition. Heck, I would not be able to pay rent with that kind of money. I kept going.

I saw another advertisement to work as a line cook, prep cook, or dishwasher. The Brewpub was a cool place to be, but when I clicked through, I saw that it wouldn't pay me anywhere near enough.

I was frustrated. I couldn't imagine why there weren't lucrative jobs. Sure, Bloomington wasn't the biggest city, but surely there was something for college students. There was probably a lot of competition, but that didn't scare me. I lived for competition.

Then something caught my eye. *Confidential job*, it said. *Contact poster for more details.* I didn't have much to lose. Everything else wouldn't work for me. I figured that I would give it a try. It could hardly be worse than the other jobs that were posted.

They had an email button, and I clicked it. I sent in the resume that I had made during my freshman year class on finding a job. I hoped that it would be good enough. I had gotten a lot of flak from the counselor when I turned in my resume, but I still had a picture of myself at the top. I felt like it personalized the resume and set it apart from the pack. Almost immediately, I got a response.

Are you available for a meeting tomorrow?

I checked my calendar. I had class from 10 AM until about 4 PM, but I could definitely meet up before or after.

Yes, I replied. *I'm available before 10 or after 4.*

Bring a suit and a swimsuit.

What? What kind of job would need both of those?

Interview

Jude

The next morning, I was wearing a swimsuit underneath my only suit. I had it for interviews, and it was a little bit dusty. I used a roller to get all the lint off of it.

I looked at myself in the mirror. I looked good enough. I brought my resume in my backpack. I was going to go straight there, and then I would go to class.

I chugged some Red Bull to give me energy, and then I went out the door.

Their office wasn't too far away from my apartment. I just had to walk down 17th St., and their office was on Walnut. If the interview wrapped up quickly, I could catch a bus down to campus.

I whistled a little bit, and then

I stopped myself. I wasn't interviewing for fun. I was interviewing so that I could stay in school. I hoped that they would pay me enough to afford to continue my education.

I opened the door to the address where I had been directed. The office looked nice, with leather chairs, but there was nobody there. There were little bells on the door, but nobody seemed to be there to answer them. I sat down in one of the leather chairs, and I stood up when I heard the door open.

There was a man with gray hair, who looked pretty wealthy. Like me, he was wearing a suit. Unlike me, the suit was definitely not a no-name brand. It fit him really well. His shoulders weren't as broad as mine, but they were definitely wider than the average width.

"Hello. You must be Jude

Adamson. I am Dennis Maven." He shook my hand, and his grip was firm. "Please, come in." He held the door open for me, and I went into the back office.

It was completely quiet back there, and I was suddenly afraid that they were going to kidnap me. Nobody knew where I was. At least if they kidnapped me, my emails would show that I met somebody here. I shivered involuntarily. How quickly would anybody notice that

I'd disappeared? Lauren Spierer still hadn't been found.

"To your left."

I looked to my left, and there was an open door. I went through it, and I saw a small office. It was full of very high quality furniture. It looked like everything was mahogany, and the finish on all of the furniture gleamed.

"Take a seat." I took my backpack off and put it next to my chair. I rolled my shoulders, which were tight. I was a little afraid, but I didn't want to show it.

He walked around his desk and sat behind it.

"Tell me a little about yourself."

I thought back to the elevator pitch that I had put together during my freshman year.

"Well, I am a finance major at Indiana University. I'm a junior, and until recently, I was on the football team."

"Why aren't you on the football

team anymore?"

I looked at him, and I squirmed a little bit in my seat. This wasn't the kind of guy that you ever lied to. He was like a principal on steroids.

"I was stupid. I went to a party, and there was alcohol. I'm only 20, and when the cops busted us, I lost my scholarship."

"Generally speaking, when you get an athletic scholarship, it's not just tuition. You get room and board as well. Is that right?"

"Yeah, I'm not really sure what's going to happen."

"I can take care of all of that for you. This job pays $1500 an hour, and I can provide your accommodation. You're on your own for taking care of utilities and groceries or whatever, but I own several properties in this area; I can put you into one that is vacant right now."

"That sounds amazing."

It sounded too good to be true. What was the catch? I had no idea what this job was, but it sounded a little bit sketchy.

"Have you ever heard of the kind of people who make fantasies come true?"

A Fairy Godfather

Jude

I frowned. "Like a fairy godmother?"

I startled a laugh out of him. "Something like that. You could become a fairy godfather. Or something like it, anyway."

"I can't do magic," I warned. "Believe me, I've read Harry Potter just like everyone else. I'm pretty solidly human."

"No magic required. I'd never ask you for something that you wouldn't or couldn't do."

"So what's the job, then?"

He opened his desk, and he took out a small brochure. It was glossy. On the front it said, *When Dreams Come True.*

"That's a pretty long name for a business."

"Yes. We normally call it Dreams. Read through the

brochure."

I opened it, and the first box that jumped out at me was "The man of your dreams." I read through the rest of the brochure, increasingly weirded out. "So, what, you have an agency for people who have weird fantasies? Do I need to buy a whip or something?"

He laughed. "No, you'll find that most women don't need the full fantasy. Female fantasies are a lot tamer than you think."

"Like what?"

"Well, sometimes women are looking for new experiences. They haven't had an opportunity to get to know a wide variety of people. Sometimes, women fantasize about gladiators. Other times, they all want a CEO to sweep them off their feet. That's what the suit is for."

"What about the swimsuit?"

"We need both of them for your

head shots."

"Head shots? What are you talking about?"

"How do you think that they make their decisions? It's mostly based on looks. Are you in?"

"Let me get this straight. You pay $1500 an hour and I can work whenever I want to? All I have to do is fulfill fantasies?"

"Yes."

I leaned back in my chair. This sounded really great except for one thing.

"Do I have to take off my pants?"

We both knew what I was talking about. "No. We technically prohibit that behavior. This is not an escort service. This is about a woman spending an evening with a gentleman whose company she enjoys."

"Sounds perfect."

"Good. I have the paperwork right here. Everything that you

need to sign is highlighted." He handed me a huge stack of papers. I flipped through them, and they seemed legitimate. I took the pen from his hand, and I signed everything.

"Let's take you for your photo shoot, and then you can be on your way. I'm sure you have class."

I followed him back. There was a very small room, and inside of it was a small photo studio. It had the fancy lighting, and it had a white backdrop.

There was a mirror to the side. He handed me a comb. "Fix your hair."

I looked in the mirror. The wind outside made my hair look a little disheveled. I combed my hair, and looked at him. He nodded in approval.

"Sit." He pointed to a small chair in the center of the room. He turned on the light, and it was blinding. I blinked a few times.

"Smile. Look like you're having fun."

It seemed kind of hard to do that when I was just stuck in the back of this office, hoping that I would get out of here in time for class. I tried to humor him, though. I thought about the time when I went for ice cream during the summer. If that didn't put a smile on my face, I didn't know what would.

He took several shots of me,

moving around the studio. He had
a lot of pictures of me from
different angles.

When he was done, he pointed
to the room next door. "We have a
changing room. I need you to put
on your swimsuit."

"Way ahead of you." I took off
my suit, and I felt like Clark Kent
emerging as Superman. I looked
at myself in the mirror and winked.
What a stud.

"Stop messing around," he said

sternly. "Look at the camera."

I looked straight into the camera lens. I had never modeled before, but it was kind of fun. It was nothing like a family picture. I thought about all those fancy advertisements for cologne, and I tried to channel that kind of man.

"Very good. Stand up. Look over your shoulder."

I turned around, and I looked over my shoulder.

"Now the other side."

I spun so that my other side was facing the camera.

"Now wink." I held my eye closed. I heard a click.

"I think that's enough for now. I'll put your profile up on the website. Do you have any special talents?"

"No." I shrugged. "I mean, football. I can't play any instruments or whatever, though."

"That's fine. Your background as an athlete is good enough.

These swimsuit pictures are going to convince plenty of customers to choose you."

I went and picked up my suit, and I put on the casual clothes that I had in my backpack. I had class in five minutes, and I was definitely going to be late.

"We'll call you when we're ready."

"Bye." I put my backpack on, and I headed to class. I miraculously caught the bus at the bus stop.

While I was clinging to one of the soft, gray plastic handles on the bus, I thought about the interview that I had just had. They were paying me a lot of money, and I hoped that somebody would choose me. It was a major plus that I didn't really have to get naked.

I walked into my Spanish literature class with a smile on my face and a bounce in my step.

Even reading *Aura*, which was the weirdest magical realism story that we had to read during this semester, didn't bring me down. I was looking forward to getting my first job. Maybe when I had to face reality and see whatever I actually had to do, this would seem more distasteful, but right now, it seemed like I had a dream job.

First Job

Jude

My phone buzzed that night.

We have a job for you. You're supposed to show up at this woman's house at 8 PM. Wear a suit. Don't be late.

I checked the time. I had an hour to get ready. I got another text telling me her address. When I read it, I whistled softly. That was a very nice part of town. I put on the suit that I had used for my interview. I knew that it was what she expected. I checked myself in the mirror. I would have to bring a mirror or something so that I could check my hair. I looked around, and then I realized I could use my phone. Thank God for front-facing cameras. I mostly used them for ChatSnap, but I was grateful for it now.

I rented a Zipcar, so I had to

pick it up in front of the student union. I drove the Zipcar to that address, using my smartphone as the GPS. I checked myself before I went in. I looked pretty much like my head shot. They hadn't done anything like hair or makeup. I should look pretty close to what they expected. I knocked on her door. Instantly, someone came.

"I was expecting you. Come in."

I went into the foyer, and I looked around. She had a really nice house. Everything was decorated in shades of gold. "You have a beautiful home." People said that to my mom all the time, and I knew that it was a compliment that women liked.

"Thank you very much. I appreciate it. Can you take off your suit jacket?"

Her request seemed pretty innocuous. I took it off, and she took it from me. She put it on a hanger in the coat closet to the side. "Excellent. Can you come into my living room?"

I followed her into her living room. I looked around. It was just as nice as the rest of the house. She sat down on a loveseat, and she patted the couch cushion next to her. "Please sit down."

I sat down, and I looked at her. She was about 10 years older than me, but she was very beautiful, more beautiful than a princess. She had long, straight, silky dark hair. She had a smile that made you want to give her one back. I smiled back at her, and I was only half conscious of doing it.

"So, what do you need me for? I didn't get a list of your fantasies from the agency, but I'm sure that you have some in mind."

"Well, I am a romance novelist. I have some questions about the heroes of my stories."

"So what does that mean for me?"

"For starters, let's just be on this loveseat. I can get some of my stories, and you can read one aloud to me. This is my editing process."

"You got my hopes up when you asked me to remove my suit jacket," I joked. "This is pretty tame compared to what I was expecting."

She laughed, and I saw that her smile lit up her eyes. "Don't worry, the fun part comes later."

She handed me a stack of paper bound together with a metal ring.

Harvey opened the door, and Jessica ran into his arms, knocking him back a step. "Where were you? I've been calling you all night. I was so worried."

"I'm fine. My phone is dead." Harvey took his phone out of his pocket and pushed the buttons. Nothing happened. "You didn't have to worry. I was fine."

"Next time that you are out of the house, please try to get in touch. I almost called the police."

Harvey shook his head. "You're sweet to worry, but it's nothing that you need to worry about." He kissed her gently, and she felt a little bit of the tension leave her shoulders.

"So what were you up to today?"

"Well, I coded a new feature."

"What does it do?"

"It permits you to dictate notes to your provider."

"Can I see it? Is it stable?"

"I haven't tested it yet, but I'm definitely going to send it to my quality assurance people soon." Jessica handed him a tablet.

"This looks pretty nice." He swiped around the tablet and tapped a few keys. "I really like the new stuff you did with the user interface." While Harvey was definitely not an expert when it came to user interface or user experience, Jessica still really appreciated his comment. Because she was working remotely, she didn't get a lot of feedback. Of course she got feedback via email, but getting feedback in person felt a lot better.

"And you? What did you do today?"

Harvey sighed. "It's the same stuff every day. I feel like I am constantly dealing with new crises. I *just wish that I had the people to handle everything that happens on a regular basis."*

"I wish that you had some good employees that could take some of the burden off of your shoulders." Jessica brought him to a loveseat. "Come here. I want to massage your shoulders."

Right then, I felt her hands go on my shoulders. She leaned forward to whisper in my ear, "Take off your shirt."

Now this was what I was expecting. I quickly unbuttoned my shirt, and I pulled it out of my pants. I put it on the armrest. Her hands were touching my bare shoulders. Her hands were warm, and it felt good as she rubbed. I felt heat spread slowly in my body, and I closed my eyes as my body relaxed. "You are really good at this."

"I should be. I have had plenty of practice."

I was embarrassed, but I had to stop myself from moaning. What she was doing with her hands just felt so good.

"It's okay to moan."

Could she read my mind? "How did you know?"

"Most of the time, people moan." She laughed gently, and I let loose. I couldn't hold back the noises that I made, and it sounded like she didn't want me to. My head fell forward, and my whole body was relaxed from her fantastic shoulder massage.

"Can you stretch out on the loveseat?"

"Of course." I moved, and she got off of the loveseat. I was face down, and she straddled my back, pressing her butt against mine. I couldn't help myself; I was getting hard. I hoped that she wanted notice, but as long as I was face down, I wouldn't have to worry about it. It was afterwards that I was worried about.

"I want you to moan."

That was not something I had a problem with. "Believe me, I will."

My moans got louder and louder as she got deeper into the massage. I was trapped under her body. She didn't weigh very much, but it kept me in place. I felt like I was sinking into the couch, and I turned my head to the side so I could breathe. My entire body was getting relaxed. Well, my entire body except for one part. One part of me definitely was wide awake. I felt myself getting drowsy. Excited about my new job, I hadn't slept much the night before. This job would permit me to cover my first tuition payment, and that meant a lot to me.

"Are you comfortable?"

I didn't want her to know just how comfortable I was.

"I'm fine," I responded.

"I think I'm about done."

"What? That's it?"

"Yes. I just wanted to know how the scene would play out. I have it straight in my head, so I think it's fine now."

"But you are paying me for an hour. It hasn't been that long."

She waved her hand. "I know that I got my money's worth. Thank you for taking off your shirt. I'll go get your suit jacket, because this is enough for tonight. I will ask for you again soon. What's your name?"

I had no idea if I was supposed to go by my own name or not, but I just went with the truth. It was a lot easier to remember my real name than any kind of fake one. "My name is Jude."

"Well, Jude, I'm Melissa." She shook my hand, which seemed silly since she had just been straddling my body while rubbing my shoulders. "I'll see you soon."

I went into the Zipcar again

totally shellshocked. I didn't know what exactly I had actually expected from my first time, but it certainly wasn't bad. I looked down at the bulge in my pants. I was softening, but just remembering how it had felt to have her body on top of mine made me want to get hard again. I drove home, thinking about this job. If every job was like this, this would be an extremely easy way to make my way through college. Heck, if easy jobs like today's were par for the course, I could make it a lifestyle. It paid a very high amount per hour, and I knew that it would be pleasurable. I guessed that most of my other clients would not try to massage me, though.

I went to my apartment, and I took off my suit. I showered, and then I opened up my laptop to work on my expository essay for the Spanish literature class discussing the Catholic symbolism in the story. The creepiest scene was the scene with the wafer. That included the way that the cats kept disappearing.

I couldn't focus, though. My first job had been such a surreal experience. I got a text on my phone.

The client is happy with your work. She tipped you $500 on top of your usual fee. You should get a notification from your bank that we've sent you the money directly.

How had they known my account number? I thought back, and I realized that I had given it to them while I had signed the paperwork.

If this was my life, it was pretty great. I just made $2000 off of less than an hour of work.

Dinner

Jude

The next night, I got another text from the agency.

Same customer wants to see you again. You need to come to her house at 8 PM.

I texted back. *I'll be there.*

They didn't say anything about the suit this time, but I figured that I should put it on again. I had gotten it dry-cleaned since last time, but I didn't really mind. I had worn it for less than an hour. I took the Zipcar again.

She opened the door before I even knocked this time.

"Oh, good, you're here. I've been waiting on you."

This time, she took me into the kitchen. "Have you eaten dinner?"

"No, I haven't."

"Sit down, please."

Whatever she had cooked

smelled very good. "It's my grandmother's recipe for chicken cacciatore. I hope you like it."

"I'm sure that I'll like whatever you cooked." I picked up my fork, and I took one bite of it. It was delicious, with the spices exploding in my mouth.

We ate in silence for a little while, although I noticed that she kept checking on me. She wasn't exactly watching me eat. She was kind of looking at the way that I interacted with my utensils. I got the impression that this was another scene, although this time she had not asked me to read her scene to her.

"So how was your day?"

What? I had no idea that she had personal interest in me. I was really here as an actor. "Oh, it was pretty normal. I don't know if you know this, but I'm a student at the university. I just go to classes and stuff."

"I remember what it was like to go to class all the time. It's a lot of fun, because your only responsibility is turning in your homework and preparing for tests." She smiled at me. "This is the best time of your life."

"I guess so." I shrugged. It didn't seem like the best time of my life. In fact, I was pretty sure that the best time of my life was when I was younger. Before I had had to worry about bills, I mostly focused on excelling on the football field. As an adult, I had a lot more concerns. I knew that a lot of people looked back on their college years with a lot of fondness, but I didn't know if I was going to be one of them, especially now that I had been kicked off of the football team. I could've understood it if I had needed to stop because of the knee injury or something, but instead, I had been disgracefully stopped. I didn't know how I would feel 10 years from now, but I knew that it would stay with me forever. How could I have been so stupid to throw everything that I had worked for away in one moment?

"Hey, are you okay?"

I forced a smile. "Of course I'm okay."

She shook her head. "You don't look like it."

"I was just thinking about losing my scholarship, that's all."

"Yes, I saw in your file that you

used to play football."

I felt my cheeks get warmer. "Yes, that's right. I used to have a football scholarship, but I messed it up."

"How did you mess it up?"

"I got caught drinking."

"Just drinking?"

I nodded. "And a little spray painting."

"That seems extreme. I mean, surely there must be consequences, but ending your scholarship seems like a pretty severe punishment for just drinking alcohol."

"Yeah, also my coach didn't want me on the team anymore." I shrugged. "That's life. Like my mom says, you can only control what you do, not what other people do."

"That's very wise for somebody so young." She cleared her throat and changed the subject. "I have a pool in the backyard. I was wondering if you could get in."

"Nobody told me to bring a swimsuit. I just wore a suit because that's what you requested last time."

"That's fine. I have a swimsuit for you."

"How do you know my size?"

"I guessed."

She went to a bag on the counter, and she pulled out a Speedo.

"I don't have anything like that

in my closet."

"Most American men don't."
She laughed. "Most American men
don't have the body to wear
something so revealing, but you
definitely do. You can put it on in
the bathroom."

She pointed to a door that was
down the hallway. "I can get the
hot tub ready."

I looked at the swimsuit. What
did they say about customer
service? The customer was always

right? I might as well put on the swimsuit. I went to the bathroom, and I took off my suit, folding it carefully. I only had one, and if I needed to use it every day, I didn't want to mess it up. I put on the Speedo. I might as well have been naked since it only protected my genitals. I felt really exposed. Also, it let out a bunch of butt cheek. I turned around and looked at myself in the mirror. I angled my body so that I could see my butt. I had never spent a lot of time looking at my ass before, but it looked really muscular. I gave myself a wink in the mirror. Looked like all the time in the gym definitely paid off.

I went out, and I went to her backyard.

Hot Tub

Jude

She had lights in her pool, so even though it was dark outside, we could still see. There was a little section that was a Jacuzzi.

By the side of the pool, I could see an ice bucket with wine in it, and there were two wine glasses. Both of them had white wine.

"Get in." The command was

soft, but I got in immediately.

It felt good to get in the warm water when the air was chilly. I sat down on the ledge, and she handed me one of the wine glasses. I drank it. It was light and fruity. "This is really good wine."

I should know. Even if I didn't really drink wine, I've been exposed to enough terrible beer to know the difference.

"This is just something I saw in my wine cellar."

"You have a wine cellar?" I thought that was something that you only saw on TV, on one of those shows about the mansions of the rich and famous.

"Yes, I do have a wine cellar."

This woman was way more fancy than I was. This wasn't the kind of thing that we had in Jasper. "So do you know a lot about wine? I have to confess, I know very little about it."

She shook her head. "No, I

really rely on the ratings online. I don't know very much about wine, only what I like."

We sank into a companionable silence. The bubbling water from the jets felt really good on my back. I had only been out of training for a couple days, but my body was already healing. As an athlete, I had been used to parts of my body hurting. When I wasn't on the field, my body actually had a chance to heal. Even in the off-season, I still ran 10 miles a day. I realized that I hadn't been running for a few days, ever since I got off the team. I made a mental note to start again. I didn't want to get fat. Just because I wasn't a football player anymore, I couldn't let myself get disgusting. I looked at Melissa. I hadn't paid much attention before, but she was wearing a very pretty pink bikini. It wasn't a string bikini. It looked more durable, but it really showcased her assets.

Whatever was happening with the neckline drew my attention to her cleavage. She was a very beautiful woman, and I felt shy suddenly. Sure, I had plenty of experience with women my age, but this was another level.

"So do you live on your own?" I wanted to make conversation. I didn't think that there was anything wrong with silence, but I might as well learn more about her, especially if she was going to be a regular customer.

"I'm on my own. I mostly write novels."

"That sounds like fun."

"It's not as much fun as you think." She smiled, and she swam towards me. "Can you put your knees together?" As soon as I put my knees together, she got in my lap. "Put your wine glass on the side." I went to obey. She put her wine glass down, too.

She leaned in, and her nose

touched mine. I cocked my neck, but she drew back an inch. "No, don't move." I got back to my original position, and she came in again. Her nose touched mine. I looked straight into her eyes. She had long eyelashes, and they were tickling me. I tried to move, but her hands pinned my upper arms, and I couldn't stop the shiver from traveling down my spine. Her nose touched my earlobe, and then she ran the tip of it down my neck.

Who knew that noses could be so erotic? I definitely hadn't before today. She touched my collarbone with her tongue, and I jumped.

"Is this okay?"

"Yeah, I just wasn't expecting it." I tried really hard to stay still. But I couldn't when she bit my neck. I bucked my hips, sending her flying out of my lap. The water slowed her down, so no harm was done, but I was really embarrassed. "I'm so sorry. I didn't mean to buck you off." I walked

forward and pulled her back into

my lap. I stroked her hair.

"It's fine," she said. She spun

around so that her ass was on top

of my erection. I knew that she

could feel it, and she rubbed up

against it, but we didn't talk. Her

hands were on my knees for

stability. It was like she was giving

me a lap dance in the water. Her

hair was soft against my chest,

and I couldn't stop myself from

putting my hands on her inner thighs and drawing her closer to me.

We both gasped as my erection pushed between her butt cheeks. I leaned forward and bit her shoulder in retribution for her biting mine earlier. She didn't seem to mind, though. She moaned in front of me, which I took as a cue to bite the other shoulder.

She spun around and took my

mouth in a wild kiss, tangling her hands in my hair. I had never been kissed like this, as if the woman in front of me would die without my kiss. She forced my mouth open with her tongue, and then her tongue was stroking deep inside of my mouth. Fire filled my body, and my hands touched every bit of her. She was melting against me, and we were grinding while we made out. I slipped a finger inside of her bikini bottoms, and I touched her down there. She didn't stop me, in fact, she urged my fingers deeper.

She broke the kiss. "More."

I used my thumb to flick her sensitive part, and she moaned in front of me. I concentrated on dropping it in a circular motion. I felt her shiver around my finger, and I kept going. Her mouth was open, and her eyes were shut. I kept rubbing her until she orgasmed. She fluttered around my finger, and I wished that it was my cock inside of her.

When she was done, she looked at me. "Would you like me to give you pleasure?"

I shook my head. "I'm good, thanks." It was too weird for me to be paid to visit her and then to get an orgasm out of it too. I liked giving women orgasms, but it seemed too intimate for her to do the same for me.

"Okay, then, we are done for this session. I definitely have enough material." She got out of my lap, and she got out of the small section of the pool. I couldn't help but admire the curve of her hips. She had a perfect body, better than most of the porn stars in the adult films that I had watched. She was very definitely a woman, not a girl, and I appreciated her curves.

When I got inside, she handed me a towel. "Here, dry off. You can get dressed in the bathroom."

I went into the bathroom, where I had left my clothes. I toweled off, and then I got dressed. When I was done, I came out of the bathroom. She was waiting by the front door. "Thank you for tonight." She seemed to hesitate for a moment, and then she came close to me. I bent down and kissed her mouth. "Thank you."

I drove home, wondering what had just happened. Had I violated any rules? No, right? All I did was wear the swimsuit that she bought for me and finger her. If she wanted it, that was okay, right?

When I got home, I saw a text.

What did you do?

I texted back. *What do you mean?*

She just paid double for that session. Was this because she had an orgasm?

I don't know why she paid double.

Well, I hope that you do as good

of a job with our other clients.

I shrugged. I didn't know how many other clients would take me into a hot tub, but I would take it. This was almost like partying, except I got paid to do it. There was literally no better job for me, and it didn't interfere with my classes. With $4500, I would be able to put down a deposit for my tuition. They had a payment plan, and I would need to go on it, because I wouldn't have enough money and time to pay my tuition in full. However, since the company was going to take up my lodging, I didn't have to worry about saving it. I knew that I needed to talk to them about my new apartment, but tonight, I was just going to relax with a cold Gatorade and catch up on some football. I had recorded a few games. I didn't need to watch game tape anymore, but I wanted to. Just because I stopped playing for this school didn't mean that I was stopped forever. When I graduated, I could definitely try to get into the NFL. Even if I wasn't picked up, I knew that there was plenty that I could do. My whole life had been football, and at worst, I could definitely coach little kids.

I realized that I needed to take a shower. I also needed to get my suit dry cleaned again. If I kept using it as my uniform, I definitely needed to make sure that it was clean. I didn't want to smell weird.

Therefore, I decided to go to the

dry-cleaner early tomorrow

morning. It wasn't too far away. In

fact, I wouldn't even need a car for

it.

I sat down and worked on

some of my calculus homework. I

knew that I didn't need to take

multivariate calculus, but it was

good to take some challenging

classes. Even though I had to keep

my grades up, as an athlete, I

wasn't really expected to take classes like this. I loved exceeding everybody's expectations. It made me feel good about my capabilities. I wasn't just a job. I would make a future for myself. I knew that my parents would be proud. It was surprisingly important, even if they weren't in contact with me that often. My parents worked so much that they didn't have the opportunity to visit me, and I didn't have a car. No matter what, though, we were tight.

What would my mom think

about what I was doing?

Gym

Jude

I felt my cheeks heat up. I didn't think that she would be proud of what I was doing, but she would definitely be proud that I was providing for myself. My parents didn't have the money to send me to college. Well, I could've stayed at home, and I could have gone to the community college.

Somehow, that never appealed to me. I knew that the University was a lot better. Indiana University had one of the biggest alumni associations in the United States, and I knew that the network would be good when I graduated. There was always the possibility that I wouldn't play football professionally, and if that ever happened, then I needed to have a set of skills. I realized that in high school, which is how I ended up at

Indiana University. It had a top 10 business school, and it offered me a full ride. I had no idea that they were so strict about alcohol consumption, but it was inexpensive enough for me to afford. I still had another year to get through, and I would need to keep this job until then. However, I knew that a business degree from them would be good enough. A lot of people from the business school ended up in Chicago, because it had a lot of jobs for young graduates. Most people try to get a job in Indianapolis, but it just didn't have enough to support the amount of people coming out of the university. Some people ended up in New York City, while others ended up in D.C. No matter what, most people tended to end up in a big city after college. For some reason, the small towns that we came from didn't have businesses that called for college graduates.

Because my head was spinning, I realized that I needed to go running. I couldn't focus on my homework, anyway.

I put on sweats and a T-shirt, and I jogged to the recreational center. The recreational center was gigantic. Sometimes, I swam, but today would not be one of those times. When I got to the entrance, they scanned my student ID card. I went upstairs to the weight room. There was a bunch of people who I saw here every day. Of course, the athletes had their own training facilities, but if you wanted to work out after hours, you came here. I saw one of my teammates, Jonathan.

"Hey man." I walked over. I hit him on the shoulder. "What's up?"

"Hey, man. I haven't seen you around."

"Yeah, I stopped playing for the team." I was surprised that the coach hadn't talked to them about it. He nodded. "Coach is a hard ass sometimes."

"You need anybody to spot you?"

"Yeah, I haven't bench pressed yet."

We went to the bench press, and I spotted him. He could press a lot of iron, but I was careful to make him do a little bit under his maximum weight. When he was sweating, he put the bar back on the rack. "Do you need spotting?"

"No," I answered. "I'm good."

"Do you want to run?"

"Sounds good." We walked over to the treadmills that were side-by-side. The recreational center played music, but he had an iPod in his pocket. He put in his headphones. We ran in companionable silence. I made sure that I was going just a little bit faster than him, but he discreetly changed the speed so that he was going just .1 mile-per-hour faster than me. We played that game until we got to the top speed that I could maintain and not fall over. We ran for an hour, until sweat was dripping on the treadmill. After an hour, I hit the stop button. I tried to catch my breath. I should have cooled down before I turned it off.

"Hey, man. I'm done for the day. Thanks for working out with me."

He hit the stop button too and

took his headphones out. He slapped my arm. "Hey, anytime. Just call me if you want to work out together." He started the treadmill again, and I went downstairs. I bought a bottle of Gatorade from the snack center, and I drink it as I walked home. I really missed the camaraderie of the football team. I wasn't close enough to anybody to see them on a daily basis, but when they would be in practice, I realized that I had been hiding from them. I was ashamed of being kicked off of the team.

I swore right then and there not to be ashamed. Sure, I had definitely messed up, but I still could hold my head up. Everybody made mistakes, and we had to learn from them. It was part of being human.

When I got to my apartment, I quickly showered. I washed off the pool water and the sweat. I had no idea what I would see the next time when I went to my client's house, but I definitely knew that I would bring another swimsuit. I really enjoyed the pool.

The first time, she had given me a massage. The second time, we had spent some time in the hot tub part of her pool. I had no idea what she had in store for the third time, but I was ready for it. If my job was to give her orgasms, I was pretty sure that I could do a good job of it. Nobody had ever complained.

Somehow, having a job made me more alert in class. I was normally sore and achy during my classes, but now that I was off of the football team, I had the time and capacity to really focus on my work. In the Spanish literature class, everybody turned around when I answered almost every question that the teacher asked. I had spent a lot of time reading the material. Before, I had read it really quickly. However, I now had the time to spend a lot of effort going through all of the material.

I wasn't surprised when I got another text from the agency.

Flowers

Jude

Go to her house at 8 o'clock.

Bring flowers.

I hadn't ever bought flowers in
Bloomington, but I figured that
there had to be florists.

I searched for one that was
open. I would pick something up
right before I went to her house.

I called ahead, and I had zero

idea what to get. They had a lot of options, and I asked them for something that would be appropriate for a friend. They assured me that they could handle it.

I waited for a little while, and then I went to the florist to pick up the bouquet. It had a bunch of flowers, except I didn't know the names of any of them. I hoped it would be good enough. They gave it to me with a little packet of crystals. The florist had a little note with it, and I brought it in my car and put it in the passenger seat. I hoped that none of the water dripped onto my seats. It wasn't even my car, so I definitely had to be careful. When I got to her door, I knocked with the bouquet of flowers behind my back. When she opened the door, I presented them to her.

"For you, my lady." I bowed.

"Is this something that Dreams

makes you do?"

I shook my head. "You asked for flowers."

"Yes, of course, I know that I asked for flowers. I meant the bow. Do they teach that to you guys?"

I shook my head. "No, this is something that I learned at Cotillion."

"You took Cotillion classes?"

I nodded. "My mom took Cotillion classes when she was a teenager, so I had to take them, too."

"That's interesting." What did she mean by that? Did she think that I was too much of a farm boy to know basic manners? My training wasn't anything that was remarkable. "Is it really so surprising?"

She laughed, and I appreciated how light and beautiful her laugh was. "No, it's not that surprising. I guess I just didn't expect it. You bow like you're an aristocrat."

I guess it was a compliment.

"So what do you want to do today?"

"Today, we're going to be in the kitchen."

I followed her into the kitchen. "Can you take off your shirt?" At least this time it was expected. I took off my shirt.

"Okay, I want you to stand right behind me when I am in front of the stove."

I stood behind her. "Okay, I

want you to put your hands on either side of my body."

I had one hand on the cold stovetop, and another hand on the countertop.

"Good. Now, lean forward so your chest is against my back."

I leaned forward, and our bodies were pressed together.

"Okay, bend at the waist, pushing me forward."

I bent over, and I could feel my body respond to the proximity to her soft curves. "Like this?"

"Yes, just like that." We were at a 45° angle, and my body was trapping her in between my lower half and the stove. I had no idea what kind of scene this was, but my body was responding to the position.

"Okay, you can let me up," she told me. "Let go of the countertop, please."

I let go, and she jumped onto the countertop. She opened her thighs. "Now come between my legs, please." I scooted forward until my belt hit the countertop. She put her arms around my neck, and I put my hands on her waist, scooting her forward. She didn't seem to mind. I brought my face close to hers, and I kissed the tip of her nose. Her eyes closed, and she made a purring sound, just like a cat.

I kissed her mouth, and the purring got louder. I didn't put my tongue inside. Instead, I stroked her back gently. My hand went to her hair, and I controlled the kiss. I still kept it soft, gentle, and slow. She seemed to like it, if the volume of her purring was any indication. I was glad that I took this job and not any of the other jobs, that was for sure. I trailed kisses to her there, and bit her earlobe gently. She shivered in my arms, and she responded by biting my neck, which made me even harder. She pressed her entire body against

mine, and I liked it. I nudged my

erection towards the sweet

juncture of her thighs.

Vanilla

Jude

I ground my body into her softness. Her breathing picked up. I buried my face in her neck, nuzzling the soft skin. She smelled like vanilla. It reminded me of baking cookies with my grandmother when I was young. For some reason, she felt like home. Her body was so soft, and she felt comfortable to hold. I leaned her back on the countertop, cradling the back of her head with my hand, so that it didn't hurt her when I lowered her. Her back was flat on the countertop. It would never work with a taller woman, but she was short enough to fit. I pushed more insistently on her lower body, and she arched her hips up. I took that as consent. I bit her neck as she moaned beneath me. I pulled down her neckline, and I kissed the tops of her breasts. Sometimes, I had mixed results. Some women didn't enjoy this kind of stimulation, but this client definitely did. I bit her cleavage, and she let out a small scream.

I found my way back to her mouth again, and we made out. This time, she shoved her tongue into my mouth as far as it would go. She pulled my hair, ripping out a few strands. It hurt, but not enough to make me stop. She kept bucking her hips into my body, and my erection was going straight between her thighs.

All of a sudden, she pulled herself upright. She used one of her hands on the countertop to push me up. "I want you to pick me up and put me on the table."

I picked her up. She didn't weigh that much. I definitely bench pressed more than her body weight. I took her to her table, which was clean. It had a tablecloth with some flowers on it. I carefully put her down. "Can the table stand up for this?"

"This table is 400 years old. It's solid wood. It's okay. They don't even make tables like this anymore. Believe me, it can hold my weight." She pulled me closer. "Now get back to what you were doing."

I obliged. Kissing her neck and rubbing my body against hers turned me on even more, raising my temperature a few degrees. When it was too much, I stopped kissing her.

"What are you doing?"

I unbuttoned my jeans, and I unzipped my zipper. My pants were uncomfortably tight, and if I was going to keep doing this, I needed to free myself.

"That's much better." I went back to what I was doing. Her responses were getting louder, and she was talking more fiercely into my body. I watched her mouth stretch open as she orgasmed beneath me. I waited for her to come down, and then I started biting the tops of her breasts. She was sensitive enough that I could tell that she was orgasmic again. Her eyes were tightly shut, and her body was shaking beneath me.

When she could talk again, she said, "Wow."

I smiled. "I'm glad you enjoyed

it."

She reached forward and unzipped my jeans. She unbuttoned them. "That was really good."

Just then, a knock came from her front door.

"I'm not expecting anybody."

She walked towards the door, and then she turned around to face me. "Just stay in the kitchen, okay?"

I nodded, and she went to the

door.

"Hello?"

She unlocked the door, and I heard a man's voice outside.

"Hello, Melissa."

The voice sounded familiar, but I could not quite place it.

"What do you want?" I hadn't realized just how much warmth was in her voice when she talked to me, but I heard the difference now. She might as well have been a polar vortex from how cold she was. It was a miracle that the entire house didn't freeze over.

"Can't I check on my wife now and then?"

"I'm not your wife. Not now, and never again."

"Oh, baby, aren't you over it now?"

"You cheated on me. How am I ever supposed to forgive you?"

"It was before we were married! It didn't count."

"A cheater is always a cheater."

She sounded mad. "You can leave now."

"Now wait a minute. I'm not ready to go yet."

"I am more than ready for you to leave." I heard the creak of the door's hinges. However, it stopped. The door banged open. It was loud enough that I wanted to help her, but I didn't know if she needed me.

"Why don't we just sit down with a nice cup of tea and talk about it? I know you love tea."

I heard footsteps coming towards the kitchen, and I was surprised to see who it was.

Interruption

Jude

It was my coach.

"What are you doing here?" we asked at the same time.

"I'm a friend of hers." I looked him up and down. "And you?"

"If you're a friend of hers, why are you shirtless?" He came close to me. "Have you been touching my woman, boy?"

"Maybe I have." I got closer to him. While he was stockier and more muscular, I had a few inches on him.

Melissa pushed us apart. "Men. Your poisoning my kitchen with your testosterone. Knock it off." She sighed. "To answer your question, he is a friend of mine. We were acting out one of the scenes in my upcoming novel. There's nothing that you need to be worried about. In fact, I would feel more comfortable if you left."

"I'm not leaving until I know what this bozo is doing here. You know that I kicked him off the team for drinking, right?"

"Hey!" I protested, "You make it sound like I'm an alcoholic."

"I don't care what it sounds like. You have no business being anywhere near my wife."

"Former wife. Remember that." She stood with her arms crossed. I could read her body language, but apparently Coach couldn't.

"One of your romance novels, then? What has this boy been doing?"

He pulled a knife from the knife block. "I remember giving you these knives as a gift when we were dating. They are stainless steel, and they never lose their edge." He raised the knife. "Yes, they are just a shiny as they always have been."

"Put that knife down!" Melissa

commanded. Coach kept the knife in his hand. "Look at the boy! You're scaring him."

I was sweating. "I'm not scared."

"Yes, you definitely are. Sit down before you fall down. And you, you can leave. What are you thinking, sitting in my kitchen and doing whatever you want? Picking up a knife? You have no business here."

"Well, Melissa, I came here to

talk to you, but I see that you are busy with your company." He sneered. "I'll come back."

"I'll see you later, then."

Coach left the kitchen, and she also followed him to the front door. When she closed it, she dead bolted it.

She walked back to the kitchen where I was still shaking. "You can put on your shirt now. I think that both of us are drained for today. I'm sorry that you had to see that.

He tends to be very possessive, even though we aren't together anymore."

"That's my coach. You were married?"

She winced. "Yes, we were married. We were only married for a month before I realized that he had slept with my best friend right before the wedding. She is no longer my best friend. And he is no longer my husband."

"That sounds hard." I hugged

her, and her arms went around my waist. I liked the way that she felt in my arms. I used my hands to trace the curves of her body. I liked the way that she nuzzled my neck. This wasn't about sex. It was about finding comfort in each other.

Speakerphone

Jude

I let go. "Are you sure that you're going to be okay?"

"Yes, of course I am. Don't worry about me."

I went back to my apartment, and I lay on my bed, thinking about the crazy coincidence. Who knew that Coach even had a wife? I definitely didn't, even if they were divorced now.

My phone buzzed. It was one of my buddies, somebody who I had known back home. I was too lazy to pick up the phone and hold it, so I put it on speakerphone.

"Hey man, what's up?"

"Hey, I was wondering if you wanted to hang out for some ice cream. Hoosier Den is open until 2 AM."

"That sounds awesome."

There was knocking at my

door.

"Hang on, I think that there's somebody here." I turned the volume on my phone all the way down.

I swung open the door, and I was greeted with a gun.

Oh man.

It was Coach. "What are you doing?"

"Keep your filthy hands off of my wife. You're not good enough for her."

"Hey, man. She's the one who invited me and you are the one who cheated on her. Surely that has to give me something of a pass."

Coach got closer to my face. "Shut your mouth. I don't want to hear your excuses. I want you to know that if I see you coming to my wife's house again, you're going to be a dead man."

It was hard to argue with a guy who had a gun in my face. I

nodded, too scared to speak

anymore. "I'm going to give you a

little reminder." With that, he

reversed his grip on the gun. He hit

me across the face with the other

end, hurting like nothing I've ever

felt before. I'd been tackled for

years. I'd been punched in the face

before, but this was another level.

Being hit with something as solid

and heavy as a gun was ten times

worse than someone else's fist.

I fell to the ground from the

force of the blow, and I felt my teeth cut the inside of my cheek. I knew I was bleeding.

"Stay away from her." He put the safety back on his gun, and he walked out.

I crawled for my phone. I turned the volume up again. "Hey, did you hear that?"

"Yeah! Who was that? Are you okay? I thought I heard somebody hit you."

"I'm okay," I lied. "He just

pistol whipped me. It's not a big deal."

"Man, you need to call the police."

I laughed darkly. "The police? What are they going to do? Who are they even going to believe? The football coach who is leading the school to victory or a football player who he just threw off the team?"

"Hey, I listened to the entire exchange. I can testify on your behalf. If you want me to, I will go to the police station with you. It's on 17th street."

I passed the station a lot of times, but I never thought that I would need to walk there. I thought about it. "That's kind of you, but I want to provoke him."

Concealer

Jude

I wasn't surprised the next day
when I got another text on my
phone. At this point, I could expect
to go to her house every evening. I
had to go to Target to buy some
concealer. I very gently brushed it
over my bruises. It could not fix all
of it, but I hoped that it would
prevent her from asking any

questions. When I was on campus, it looked like I'd been in a bar fight. Lots of people had slapped me on the back and said good job man. They had no idea where I got it from. But once I went to her house, she had a good idea of someone who would touch me like that.

I drove to her house, and I thought about leasing a car. Maybe I couldn't afford a full car right now, but if I didn't have to pay for rent, I would have enough money for a car payment. I didn't need anything flashy, so I would probably choose something small and reliable. I thought of a Toyota Corolla, but it always seemed like the Toyota cars were too small. For trucks or gas guzzlers, I'd grown up with everybody in my area having one. I would need to choose a car that fit what I did now.

She was on the front steps of her house waiting for me. The

second she saw me, her eyes popped open.

"What happened to your face?"

I touched it. I was surprised that she could see so quickly through the concealer.

"Nothing," I shrugged.

"Bruises that large are not nothing. Come inside." I walked behind her into the house, and she led me into the kitchen. She wet the towel, and she very gently brushed itover my cheek, rubbing off the concealer. She gasped in a breath when she realized how bad the damage was. It was black in the center and green around the edges.

"It doesn't hurt," I lied.

"Who did this to you?"

I was silent.

"I know the answer to that question."

She frowned. "You're not in any shape to get up to anything tonight. You should go home.

You're hurt."

"No," I protested. "I'm fine. I just hit my face on something hard, that's all. Believe me, in football, I've had worse."

"Go home," she told me more firmly.

"Please," I told her, "I need this job."

I guessed it hadn't occurred to her that I needed the income that she provided, but her whole posture softened then.

"You can stay. But you're going to rest, and you're going to take pain medication. That's not negotiable."

"That's fine by me," I told her. "Just point me to a bed and some meds." I tried not to take more pills than absolutely necessary, but I figured that if someone else made me take them, they were absolutely necessary.

She had a guest bedroom on her ground floor, and I took off my shoes before getting into the bed. It was soft but firm, with something like a TempurPedic mattress. I sank, but it had plenty of support.

She left and returned quickly. In one hand was an ice pack; in the other, she held a bottle of Aleve.

"What do you like to drink? I don't have a huge variety, I'm afraid. I have apple juice, orange juice, or water."

"What? No milk?" I tried to

joke, but smiling hurt.

She noticed. "Don't smile," she snapped. "I'm getting you apple juice." She went into the kitchen. I could hear her open the fridge, and she came back after she poured me a glass.

"Take your meds, boy."

"Yes, nurse." I winked at her.

She smiled, and she got into bed next to me. She curled up on my shoulder, on the opposite side of where I was hurt. I slipped my arm around her, resting my hand at her waist. She was a sweet armful, and I'd appreciate lying in bed beside her a lot better if I weren't hurt. She was treating me like a bird with a broken wing, and I was a man with a simple bruise on my face. My cock didn't care, honestly. I was pitching a tent right now, and somehow it didn't make me uncomfortable. If I were in public, I would have to hide it. But right now, in this bed, I felt myself getting harder and harder. I knew that she could definitely see it if she looked. I didn't know if her eyes were open or closed.

"Are you awake?"

She pushed up my shirt, which answered that question.

Shirtless

Jude

Her hand traveled down my stomach, tracing the ridges of my abs. I saw her follow her hand with her tongue.

I gasped harshly. She had reached the bottom of my abs, and she was now biting the delicate skin beneath my belly button.

"Are you ready for this?" she

asked me.

"Ready for whatever you want," I replied.

She responded by unbuttoning my jeans and pushing down my boxers. She definitely knew what she was doing. They were pushed down and off my feet in what felt like a second. Then I was there with my shirt pushed up to my armpits and my lower half totally bare.

"Get naked," she commanded. I

sat up and pulled off my shirt.

"As the lady commands."

She pulled me to the edge of the bed. "I want you to put your hands behind your head. Maybe we can try some other stuff in the future, but for right now, this is the position that we need to take."

I put my hands behind my head.

She knelt on the ground between my legs, and it was one of the most erotic sights in my entire life to see her head between my legs. I closed my eyes, though, when she touched the tip of my cock with her tongue. It felt so good, and I felt my cock getting longer and harder.

"That's right," she praised. "That's good."

I was beyond speech. I urged her to take more of my cock by pushing my hips up, but her hands came to force my hips down.

"Be still," she said sharply.

"How can I go down on you if you can't stay still?"

"I'll try," I promised.

"You'll do it, or this whole thing stops."

She went back to sucking on my cockhead. I wanted to move in the worst way, but I knew that I could not. My whole body was vibrating with the force of holding back. I was sweating, and my breathing was getting harder and harder. When she did a long lick from the base of my balls to the top of my cock, I couldn't hold back anymore. I exploded all over her; I could not stop myself.

She took all that come like a complete champion, sucking down every drop, licking up everything. I was still shaking on the bed when she shoved me back so that my back was on the sheets.

"My turn."

Queen

Jude

She got naked, and she sat on my face. I'd never had a woman do this before, but it was an easy way to access her pussy. She tasted sweet, like she smelled. It was a hint of vanilla and a whole lot of woman. I knew how to touch her clit with my nose while my tongue gave her pleasure, and she was rocking hard against my face as I slowed the pace down, giving her long, slow licks.

She screamed, and her lower lips fluttered against my face; I didn't stop, just licking her again and again.

She got off of my face, and she curled back up against my shoulder. This was a dramatically different position than it had been earlier tonight, now that we had given each other orgasms.

"Was that good for you?" I whispered.

"Good? Good is almost an insult. That was fantastic, Jude, just fantastic." She kissed me lightly on my mouth. I could taste myself, and I was sure that she could taste her own come. She forced my lips open, and she tasted more of her pussy.

"Mm, so good."

Now she was straddling my body, her mouth still attached to

mine. My cock sprang back to life as I thought about the way that her legs were split above me. It wanted to be inside of her in the worst way, but I told it to chill out. It was enough that we were getting kissed by an absolute expert.

She started grinding her ass against my erection, kissing me, and then breaking the kiss to push her body down. She was swinging herself from her shoulders, and I loved it. She definitely knew what she was doing, and I couldn't be more amazed. I could feel just a hint of her dampness touch me every time that she moved, and my dick couldn't take it. I spurted precome. I was done waiting.

I flipped her so that she was on her back. I was grateful that the bed was big enough for us to wrestle a little bit.

She didn't protest when I put her legs over my shoulders.

"I'm going to take you deep," I

told her.

"Yes."

I probed her wetness with my finger, but all I found was slick, wet heat. She was ready for me. I slammed into her. Slow, sweet love would happen another time. Right now, it felt like I would die if I wasn't coming into her body.

I used her legs as a base as I plunged in and out of her delicious body. My eyes closed, and I could hear her moaning beneath me. If I had the presence of mind, I'd be caressing her clit right now, but I couldn't do it. All I could think of was driving my cock inside of her again and again. She was mine in an elemental way. Maybe it was the way that she had cared for me. I understood now why the naughty nurse idea was so popular.

I came close to orgasm, but I pulled out.

"Don't stop," she pleaded. I didn't say anything. I flipped her so that she was on her stomach.

"Get on your hands and knees." It didn't even sound like my voice at this point. She complied with the deep command.

I spent a few seconds looking at the arch of her back and her curvy ass. I bit it hard, hard enough to leave a mark. She seemed to love it, though, pushing her ass back at me.

I took that as consent. I resolved to go a little slower this time, now that the madness wasn't consuming me. I touched the tip of my cock to her entrance.

"You like this?"

"Yes," she confessed softly. "Yes."

"You want it?"

"Yes."

I pushed in an inch. "Like this?"

"More!" She tried to push her hips back, but I was faster than her. My reaction time was what kept my cock from re-entering her body entirely.

"Are you sure?" I smiled, teasing her a little.

I shouldn't have teased her. She spun around, and she all but shoved me on my back. I was startled as she straddled my body and shoved my cock inside of her.

We both moaned, and, besides her muscles fluttering on my dick, she was quiet for a second. She was still, and then she started moving on me.

She had her hands on my pecs in order to stabilize herself, and I helped her as she moved. My hands were guiding her hips up and down on me, and I loved the sounds that she was making. The scent of sex filled the air, and I knew that this was the best I'd ever have.

I spurted some precome inside of her, and she picked up the pace. She bent low now, and she was riding me as hard as a jockey on the leading racehorse I didn't know how long I could hold back with my body pulsing for release, but I didn't want to come before she did.

She came apart on top of me, gasping for air, arching her back.

So I took that as permission to come myself. She was still quivering as I shot my load inside of her.

As the sex fog cleared from my brain, I had the presence of mind to ask her, "Are you on birth

control? We didn't use anything.

I'm clean, and I can show you the

medical paperwork."

Shower

Jude

"I'm on birth control. I have to use it to control my amenorrhea." She smiled. "I'm clean, too. I haven't had a sexual partner since my cheating ex-husband, and it's just fine for you to be inside of me bare."

"If that's the case, then I'd like to take a shower. With you, if you catch my drift."

She smiled, and she pulled me towards the bathroom.

She was a small woman, but every bit of her body screamed just how confident she was. She was a marvel to me. I'd never met anybody like her. She was at home in her own skin in a way that I admired.

She turned on her shower and we stepped inside. The warm water felt like a benediction. She got to her knees, and she started sucking my cock. It was semi-hard from watching her walk into the shower, and now it was hard enough to drive nails from the feeling of her hot, warm mouth touching it.

She tugged at me with her hand, and then it was all over. I filled her mouth with spurt after spurt of my come. When I was done, she got to her feet.

"I want to wash you."

She reached for a loofah, and

she squirted some kind of shower gel on it. I watched as she touched my entire body with the soapy loofah. I didn't know that I could get turned on by somebody cleaning me up, but my erection was definitely trying to make a comeback. She worked her way up from my ankles to my chest. When she got to my face, I stole the loofah from her.

"My turn."

She gracefully allowed me to do

the same to her. I rubbed the soapy loofah over her slick, soft skin. She was beautiful, like one of those pagan fertility goddesses. I kissed the areas that I was touching right before I cleaned them. I spent extra time on her breasts, making sure they were totally clean. The water washed away all the soap, and both of us were totally clean.

I knelt between her legs, just as she had knelt for me. I coaxed her clit out, and I sucked on it gently. Her knees buckled a little bit, and I kept her standing with my hands on her hips. She bucked wildly into my mouth, and the scream that she gave told me that she was climaxing. I waited while she shivered in my hands, then I stood up.

"Turn around." She spun, facing the wall and bracing herself with her hands.

"This one's going to be rough,"

I warned. "I'm not going to hold back."

"Take me."

I thrust into her with one push. Maybe she should have been wider at this point, but she felt just as tight as she had the first time that I'd had her tonight. I was glad to finally have sex with her. I pushed her hard against the wall, trapping her luscious body between me and the tile. I pounded inside of her small body, but she

took every thrust and pushed back
to give as good as she got. I knew
that she could match me, no
matter what I did.

I didn't want to come inside of
her in the shower.

"I want you in a bed." I slipped
out, then I turned off the water. I
swung low, and I threw her over
my shoulder. We were both wet
and slippery from the shower, but I
managed.

I walked back into the

bedroom, and I threw her on the bed. I prowled above her as I leaned down to kiss the soft curves of her breasts. When we were in the shower, I was a little too tall to do them justice. I needed to have her on her back in this bed, but I was going to give her an orgasm by worshiping her breasts alone, with no other stimulation.

I started by biting in a circle around the edges of her breasts, slowly spiraling inwards. I didn't touch her nipples. She was

writhing beneath me on the bed,

arching her back for me.

I finally bit her, hard, and she

screamed. I kept biting her,

knowing that I was definitely

leaving marks and not caring at

all. She creamed again, arching

her back off the bed in a huge bow,

and I was thrown clear. I watched

as she gasped her way through a

climax.

I pulled her on her side when

she was still recovering, and I put her top leg on top of mine. "I can't wait to be inside of you." I put my chin on her shoulder, and I guided my cock into her slick heat. She moaned as I slid inside. It was a smooth glide, because she was so wet. I brought my hand in front to rub her clit and to control the motion of her pelvis. She felt like heaven.

I pounded into her, glad that she wasn't a stick figure. When I'd had sex with skinny girls, it felt like falling on a pile of broomsticks. It wasn't particularly pleasant. But with this woman's sweet ass, I felt comfortable pounding into her as hard as I could go. She took it and loved it.

I pulled out as soon as I got close to orgasming. "I want to try something."

Sometimes, when I had a spare moment, I would visit the IU Art Museum. It wasn't too far away from class, and it was a place to seek some quiet and get my head on straight. There was a Hindu statue of two gods there. The man was on the bottom, and the woman was on top. But of them were sitting tailor-style on top of each other.

I sat on the bed, and I pulled her into my lap. "I want you to cross your legs behind my back." She did, and I was ready to enter her again. I slipped right back inside, and she was fantastic. Just sweet and perfect in my arms. Who knew that it would feel this great? I definitely hadn't. She was a wonderful woman, and it was even better because I knew that she was mine. In the depths of my soul, I felt my body claim her forever.

It was slow and gentle like this. We kissed, and we kept our eyes open. We stared at each other in complete silence while our bodies did the talking. I wanted to go like this for the entire night. Her chest was rubbing mine as her arms were around me, pulling me close, and I knew that I'd never find better. She was the sweetest sin, and I couldn't get enough.

We rocked like that for an amount of time that could never be counted. When her mouth slipped open, I knew she was orgasming. The orgasm took us both like a sudden spring shower: gentle, but startlingly violent once it started.

I poured more come than I even knew my body could produce into her when we orgasmed that time.

I was so exhausted by my orgasm that I pulled her into my arms. I tucked her into the curve of my body, holding her close.

"You're fantastic," I told her softly. My body wouldn't let me stay awake any longer, and I fell quickly into a divine sleep.

Coffee

Jude

When I woke up, I could smell coffee. My body was sore. I had used muscles that were never used on the football field, that was for sure.

I walked into the kitchen naked. I wasn't ashamed of my body. And when we'd spent last night exploring each other in great detail, I didn't think that she would mind. My morning wood bounced a little with each step. I was hoping that she would help me take care of it.

"Good morning," I called out. She was cooking pancakes. "Smells great." I settled my hands around her small waist and hugged her tight. "Are you cooking breakfast for me?"

"Yes." She spun around and tilted her face up. I surprised her by picking her up off her feet and kissing her soundly.

She broke the kiss. "Put me down! The pancakes will burn."

"That's a risk I'm willing to take." I kissed her again, and this time she didn't stop me.

When my mouth started getting dry, I put her back on her feet. She flipped a pancake, and I saw that it was well-done, bordering on burnt. I grinned. I'd eat whatever she cooked me. I saw now the appeal of bending her over the stove, though I didn't think that it was a safe idea when the burners were on. I mentally filed that away for another time.

I was sitting at the table, naked, when she brought two dishes of pancakes to me.

"Sit in my lap," I urged.

She shook her head. "If I sit in your lap, I don't think that we are going to be eating."

I smiled. She had only spent

one night with me, but she already knew what it would be like.

She had maple syrup on her table, and I poured some on her pancakes before eating mine. The pancakes were tender enough, despite being well done, that I could use just my fork. They were so fluffy, and I moaned.

"You're a good cook."

"Thank you."

I finished all the pancakes on my plate, and then I watched her finish up. I grabbed the bottle of maple syrup. "I've got plans for this." She smiled.

"Lead the way."

I picked her up bridal style this time, and we headed for the bedroom again. I had no idea if I had classes or not today — dimly I thought that it was Saturday — but I didn't care. I was going to use this maple syrup on her come hell or high water.

I sat her on the bed, then I

pushed her gently backwards.

"Be still, okay? If you move, you're going to make a mess."

I drizzled the maple syrup down the center of her body. She looked good like that, sweet maple syrup glistening on her beautiful skin. I started at the top, licking down her sternum, past her breasts, down her stomach. I finally got lower, and I started lapping at her clit.

"You're sweeter than any

syrup." I felt like I couldn't get enough of her juice. She tasted so good.

I pushed her thighs wider, and I got into it. She was moaning on the bed, and all of a sudden, her climax hit both of us. I was humping the bed, trying to find some relief, and she wasn't even trying. She was flying high.

I slammed her face down on the bed, basically flat. She liked it however I gave it to her, hard and rough, slow and sweet. I knew that this time, I'd go hard. I pulled her legs up beneath her so that she was kneeling, and I slammed into her. My front was plastered to her back, and she was moaning under my body as I rocked into her again and again.

I spurted some precome, but I wasn't done. I bit her shoulder, and her entire body shivered. It was enough to make me blow my load.

I heard some loud knocking on her door.

"Don't answer it," I whispered. She didn't pay attention to me.

"I better go see who that is."

She threw on a fancy dress from the closet — which seemed to be full of formal gowns — and she went to the door.

"What is it?"

It was Coach again.

"Why are you wearing that? Did you just get home from an

evening out?"

"It's none of your business. Seriously, just go." She tried to close the door, but Coach pushed his way inside despite what she wanted. I was sitting on the bed in the guest bedroom when Coach pulled his gun out of his holster.

If I had been a second slower, the end of my life would've been right there. Coach took in the rumpled bed sheets and the smell of sex, and he fired on me.

I tackled him like I'd always practiced, hitting low and taking him down. I wrestled him for control of the gun, and I was successful in pushing it out of his hand.

He was older and wilier than me, but I was taller and in better shape. I pushed him down so that he couldn't stop me from returning his punch with interest. I loved the way that it sounded when my fist met his face. Yeah, it wasn't going to be the same as pistol whipping him, but it was definitely enough for me.

I heard the sound of sirens. The police station must have been right by her house. I hadn't noticed her calling the police, but I'd been occupied.

He was limping as he ran out the back, smashing his way through the back door. I did a flying tackle to get him into the pool, and the splash that we made was definitely huge. It was hard to wrestle in the water, and I went for the side. He did, too.

"Freeze!" There were two policemen there with their guns drawn. "Hands up!"

"This is a misunderstanding," Coach said, his tone conciliatory. "I was just trying to help this poor, misguided boy; he attacked me."

"That's not what happened at all." Melissa came out of the house. "It's all documented in the 911 call."

"Sir, we're going to have to take you both in. There's clear destruction of property. We'll take statements from both of you."

Epilogue

Melissa

The police involvement was the final touch. He couldn't keep it up, not with Jude and I singing the same song. He got locked up, and he lost his position at the university.

Jude gave up being a

Dreamboat, and instead he just stuck with the woman of his own dreams. Maybe other relationships founded on hot sex wouldn't last, but I knew that ours would.

I funded the rest of Jude's time in school. My parents weren't all that happy that I was dating a man who was a decade younger than me, but they got over it when they realized how in love we were.

We got married after Jude graduated. Jude started a small

financial advisory firm, and he

worked from our home. Jude and I

loved eating lunch together and

having time to get in a little

playtime.

Alyse Zaftig is a romance author who loves to write about women who break the mold. Sassy heroines are her favorite.

Learn more about Alyse Zaftig at http://zaftigpublishing.com